Dog in a Dress

and

Run, Tom, Run!

By **Katie Dale**

Illustrated by **Giusi Capizzi**

The Letter I

Trace the lower and upper case letter with a finger. Sound out the letter.

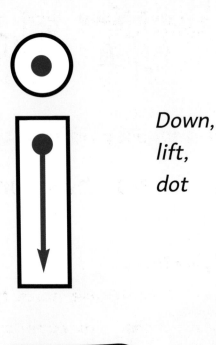

Down,
lift,
dot

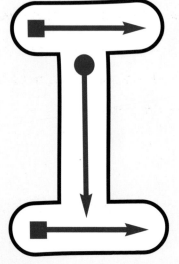

Down,
lift,
across,
lift,
across

Dog in a Dress

RC

and

Run, Tom, Run!

Maverick

Early Readers

'Dog in a Dress' and 'Run, Tom, Run!'
An original concept by Katie Dale
© Katie Dale

Illustrated by Giusi Capizzi

Published by MAVERICK ARTS PUBLISHING LTD

Studio 3A, City Business Centre, 6 Brighton Road,

Horsham, West Sussex, RH13 5BB

© Maverick Arts Publishing Limited July 2017

+44 (0)1403 256941

A CIP catalogue record for this book is available at the British Library.

ISBN 978-1-84886-290-6

www.maverickbooks.co.uk

This book is rated as: Red Band (Guided Reading)
This story is decodable at Letters and Sounds Phase 2.

Some words to familiarise:

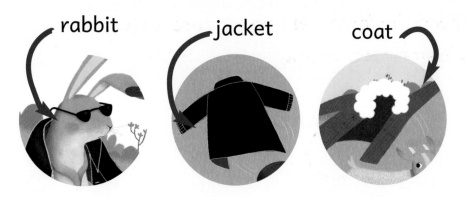

rabbit
jacket
coat

High-frequency words:

the   is   a   it   no   has   on   my

Tips for Reading 'Dog in a Dress'

- *Practise the words listed above before reading the story.*
- *If the reader struggles with any of the other words, ask them to look for sounds they know in the word. Encourage them to sound out the words and help them read the words if necessary.*
- *After reading the story, ask the reader whether they remember which clothes each animal was wearing.*

Fun Activity

Can you think of any other animals wearing silly clothes?

Dog in a Dress

The duck is wearing a red sock.
Is it the duck's sock?

The rat has a big hat on.

The cat is wearing a yellow cap.

The dog likes wearing the blue dress.
Is it the dog's dress?

The rabbit has
a black jacket on.
Is it the rabbit's jacket?

No!

What is the goat wearing?

The Letter W

Trace the lower and upper case letter with a finger. Sound out the letter.

Down,
up,
down,
up

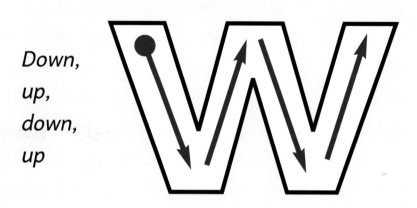

Down,
up,
down,
up

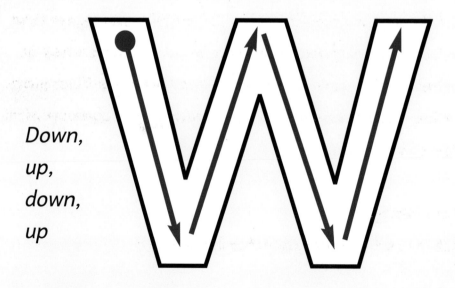

Some words to familiarise:

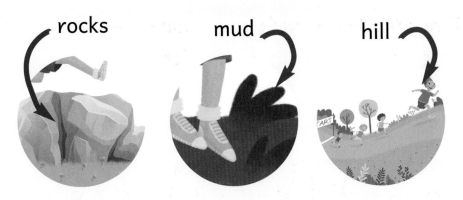

rocks   mud   hill

High-frequency words:

I the into a it to was up

Tips for Reading 'Run, Tom, Run!'

- Practise the words listed above before reading the story.

- If the reader struggles with any of the other words, ask them to look for sounds they know in the word. Encourage them to sound out the words and help them read the words if necessary.

- After reading the story, ask the reader if they remember what Tom saw on his run.

Fun Activity

Ask the reader what sports they like to play.

Run, Tom, Run!

Tom likes to run.

Tom likes to win.

Tom runs up the hill.

Tom runs over the rocks.

Tom runs into the mud.

Tom runs across the sand.

Tom runs
under the net.

Tom runs over the log!

Splash!

"I did not win. But it was
a fun run!" says Tom.

Book Bands for Guided Reading

The Institute of Education book banding system is a scale of colours that reflects the various levels of reading difficulty. The bands are assigned by taking into account the content, the language style, the layout and phonics.

Maverick Early Readers are a bright, attractive range of books covering the pink to purple bands. All of these books have been book banded for guided reading to the industry standard and edited by a leading educational consultant.

For more titles visit:
www.maverickbooks.co.uk/early-readers

 Pink

 Red

 Yellow

 Blue

 Green

 Orange

 Turquoise

 Purple

Book Band
Red

Dog in a Dress and Run, Tom, Run!	978-1-84886-290-6
Buzz and Jump! Jump!	978-1-84886-250-0
Bam-Boo and I Wish	978-1-84886-251-7
Sam the Star and Clown Fun!	978-1-84886-288-3
Seeds and Stuck in the Tree	978-1-84886-289-0